ON THE WINGS OF MY DRAGONFLY

ON THE WINGS
OF MY
DRAGONFLY

MARIA GARAY REYNOLDS

On The Wings Of My Dragonfly

Copyright © 2020 by Maria Garay Reynolds. All rights reserved.

No part of this publication may be reproduced, stored in a retrieval system or transmitted in any way by any means, electronic, mechanical, photocopy, recording or otherwise without the prior permission of the author except as provided by USA copyright law.

The opinions expressed by the author are not necessarily those of URLink Print and Media.

1603 Capitol Ave., Suite 310 Cheyenne, Wyoming USA 82001
1-888-980-6523 | admin@urlinkpublishing.com

URLink Print and Media is committed to excellence in the publishing industry.

Book design copyright © 2020 by URLink Print and Media. All rights reserved.

Published in the United States of America

ISBN 978-1-64753-417-2 (Paperback)
ISBN 978-1-64753-418-9 (Digital)

18.09.20

CONTENTS

Acknowledgement vii
Preface ix
Chapter 1   On the wings of my dragonfly 1
Chapter 2   Back to my present life 9
Chapter 3   Without filters 13
Chapter 4   Living in the moment 17
Chapter 5   New Born till age Seven 21
Chapter 6   The Road Back to Wholeness 25
Chapter 7   Knowledge within 29
Chapter 8   Healing from the Universe and the Quantum Field 31
Chapter 9   Sharing my past and my future 33
Chapter 10   Interweaving Life Experience to Reach 35
Chapter 11   Meditations for your Heart and Well-being 39
Chapter 12   We are Spiritual Beings with Colorful Auras 43

ACKNOWLEDGEMENT

This book was inspired by my great-grand boy, Charles Ulysses Ross III. On his 3rd birthday party, we talked and played rolling around the floor when he began telling me his story about his spirit friend. Talk to your little ones and believe them when they share what they see and know that will give them confidence because they were heard and validated. Remember, their truth is pure, funny, exciting; it is not their imagination; it is there life as they are experiencing it.

My story is not the important part of this book, it is just a spring board into your own story to help you remember your baby story.

PREFACE

I dedicate this book to Charles Ulysses Ross III; He took me on a journey and I hope he takes you on your own childhood memories. Believe what they see and enjoy ; the pure love they give, join them in their world. All my teachers and students have given me great knowledge and I still continue learning every day. I am sharing my Charles' story, it reminded me of and opened a conversation into my childhood.

CHAPTER 1

ON THE WINGS OF MY DRAGONFLY

By Maria Garay Reynolds

Early Saturday morning, the sun was just rising over the crest of our hill where my house sits. The sun was shining bright as a spotlight into the bedroom window. Moving my arm across my eyes covering the sun while slowly opening my eyes wide open, the first thing that came to mind was a dragonfly, a big bright beautiful dragonfly of multicolor. Was it a dream or a memory? Quickly my mind was flooded with thoughts of today's big birthday party.

Moving swiftly out of bed, I started heading for the bathroom. Today was a big day; It was my great-grandson birthday and his older sister's birthday as well.

My voice echoed through the house humming while walking to the bathroom having already picked out a colorful top and white jeans and carefully laying them out the night before. Turning on the shower and waiting for the water to be just right, I stepped into the water letting the hot water flood my body. The water was so delicious, I continued to hum, not wanting to turn off the cascading water, thinking about the dragonfly.

Finally forcing myself to turn the water off, I grabbed the towel wrapping it around me. The towel swallowed my small frame. I was careful not to step on the towel while stepping out.

Dancing into the bedroom, I finished drying off, and draped my wet towel over the brown hamper. A memory of buying the hamper in Deming, New Mexico crossed my mind for a short second. Silly how those kinds of thoughts can pop up out of nowhere. We have been back in California for six years. I moved out of those thoughts slipping into my clothes, looking in the full-length mirror. Twirling a couple of times to make sure, the clothes looked right on me.

I continued across the room to my makeup vanity chair to dry my hair and apply some light makeup. I finished and put everything away, making sure the hair dryer and curling iron were turned off and cooled down. Excitement rose through my heart causing me to laugh out loud, making a small dance moves with happiness. My heart was so full I began to dance again, laughing in pure joy; today was definitely one of those heart tickling days.

My husband, Robert, and I loaded the gifts and the food into the car. We took the Chevrolet because it had more space for the gifts and food. We had purchased the Chevy so we had a vehicle especially for our four dogs when they needed to be groomed or visit the vet and other occasions like today.

Excitement mounted again; family gatherings are very important to us. We double checked to make sure we did not forget anything. I closed the trunk, walked around to get in, buckled in then we headed to Sacramento. My great grand daughter was turning ten years old today. It was a very important day. We were also celebrating my three-year-old great-grand son's birthday as well.

As we parked at to our granddaughter's house, I checked my wrist watch. We had arrived on time. Knocking on the door would change my life in a wonderful exciting way I never expected.

We heard a voice inviting us to come in. The front door opened and we walked into my granddaughter's house. We were greeted with big smiles and I collected lots of hugs. My granddaughter took the gifts, placed them on the table.

As soon as my great- grandbaby boy saw me, his eyes sparkled big and bright, smiling wide he ran towards me as fast as his little legs would carry him yelling, "Granny." He jumped up into my arms giving me kisses with a big hug, holding my neck tight. Such love from my three-yearold great grandbaby boy is the most beautiful experience of pure love in the world. My great granddaughter came around the door and gave me a big sweet hug. She is a gentle soul with a lot of grace and warmth in her smile. I admire her kindness with her brother and sister. She helps her mom with the children and has great grades at school. Quiet and very intelligent.

Chatter and background noises were loud. I spotted my great-grandson across the living room; he was playing and talking to someone. Curious, I walked over and sat down on the floor across from him. I picked up a toy car and began playing with him.

He kept looking behind me and talking. I asked, "Who are you talking to?" He pointed his tiny little finger at the wall, saying over there. We fell to the floor laughing. It did not take long before he was telling me all about his friend that came to visit him. I asked him what his name was, he shrugged his shoulders moving his head from side to side saying, "I do not know." I do not like him.

My next question was why? He was quick to tell me that his friend was not nice to him. He pointed, "He over there." I looked up and could only see the outline of a young boy that appeared to be around five or six years old. So, I asked him to tell me more.

After a long conversation of chatter of a three-year-old, of which I did not understand most of it, except for a few words here and there. My reply was, "Really," and his little head moved up and down.

I began to ask him questions to see if I understood what he was saying. Simple questions that he could answer with a yes or no. Finally, I got the whole story.

I put him on my lap and told him that next time he shows up and is mean to you, tell him "Go away" and that he is not welcome here any longer. I instructed him, "Tell him in a big loud voice."

I knew it was the spirit of a boy. Not a make-believe boy, but a real spirit. Before I stood up to visit the rest of the family, I told him, "Remember tell him, 'No, go away'." He gave me big hug and off he went to play.

It was a perfect day- filled with fun, lots of great food, with all the children and their kids. It was getting late in the day so we said our goodbyes, headed home up the hill to Placerville. During the trip back home, thoughts of all the fun and conversations ran through my mind.

That night while getting ready for bed, thoughts once again flooded my mind of my wonderful day. Then in a flash, a memory of my own childhood journey of spirit friends, and the not-so friendly spirits that appeared before me. I turned and said to my husband, "Well, we have another child that sees spirits."

I turned over and said good night. I felt his hand on the back of my shoulder, and he replied, "You do have a lot of children that are intuitive."

The conversation with my great-grandson about his boy spirit played in my mind. I could not sleep so I got up, went into my art studio, sat in my soft brown recliner chair closing my eyes. It did not take long sitting in the quiet of the night before an avalanche of old memories came up.

My brothers came to mind first, how we played cowboys and Indians; those memories opened the gates of my childhood.

I was transported back in time to my baby version of myself. Smiling with excitement, looking at myself in my mind's eyes big screen. Wow! There I was, playing in my make-believe world, peeling back the years, back to my levee at Elkhorn Ferry. Looking at myself, running up and down the steep levee pretending I was flying with my arms stretched out. All of a sudden, I could feel the air moving around me and could feel myself flying while sitting in my chair.

Oh, those sweet memories of pure joy continued playing in my mind's eye. Those magical years of pure creativity were mixed with pure innocence. I had two spirits visit my bedside when I was very young. I did not remember my age but remembered the lady in her white flowing dress and the child beside her was also floating above the floor. Her white flowing dress was magically long and sparkly. She moved about one foot above the floor holding the small girl spirit's hand. I was amazed the child stood just at her side. Over time I also saw them both outside as well. I would only see them from time to time. I was never afraid of them; I just thought they were friends, even to this day. The last time I saw them was around 1977, standing next to the road on my way from Reno, Nevada to the hospital in Sacramento, California where my father was. I heard the message like a whisper in my ear that my father was fine, and to slow down and drive careful. (Quickly my thoughts moved back to my memories of my dad and growing up.) Suddenly the voice again whispered slow down and as I turned on a upcoming curve the lady in her long white dress was in front of me. I quickly put my foot on the brakes and slowed down, relaxed and focused on the curved road ahead.

The drive was very long and intense with me trying to focus on the white line. My mind started wondering with thoughts of my dad not living through whatever he was going through at the hospital before I got there. My heart was beating so hard I thought it would go through my chest. Suddenly memories growing up all of a sudden were right outside my car window. My home on the ranch where I was raised with all its magical wonder of the Sacramento river with all its beauty just across our old home.

I opened the car window and immediately, vividly I could smell the fresh grass and wild flowers springing all around me. I was transported back in time. The wild flowers were yellow, purple, and white and the fragrance was sweet and wonderful. Many types of weeds were growing tall everywhere. They were green to dark green. Some were round looking like snakes, and the blades of grass were thin and some round while others were tall and looked like little trees - so many different colors of green with touches of yellow. I lay on the tall grass that felt like a soft blanket. I sank into the soft grass and the weeds were so tall the wind blew right over me keeping me warm and safe. The smells were like no other. My forest was full of alien life forms and strange animals that I alone knew. As my journey continued to the hospital, great fragrances continued along with different colors that tasted so delicious. Even till this day, color to me is so delicious.

A perfect wonderland continued unfolding before my mind's eyes. I could still hear the buzzing sounds of bees and other insects. I laid still enjoying them. The insects had different bright colors and their own unique sound. I loved when the butterfly landed on me. I would hold my breath so it would not leave me. So exciting! I can still feel and hear myself laughing in pure joy. The only insect I feared was the bumblebee; I would scream like a banshee. They looked so big; I was sure they would kill me. My world was filled with wonder and bright beautiful color, even the bumble bee had bright, bright yellow and black colors. I rolled up the windows and continued on to the hospital were my father was. Thanking my angel that helped keep me stay safe.

I walked into my father's room at the hospital; he looked pale but sounded good. I talked to his doctor, and he assured me my father was fine. Visiting was short as other family members were waiting to see him. Later that evening, I stayed with my youngest brother in Sacramento for a couple of days until my father was home. It was time for me to head home back to Reno, Nevada. Feeling full of joy and excitement to see my children, started my trip back cruising up Highway 50.

Amazing how my great-grand boy triggered so many childhood adventures. I got up from my chair made myself a cup of coffee and watched the sun come up, refusing to give up my exciting memories as a child playing in my world on the levee at Elkhorn ferry. That levee was across my parents' house, where I played in a truly magical world of my own for many years.

Many nights I danced with my fairy friends falling down, rolling in laughter on soft tall green grass. Still pretending some of the plants where from outerspace or were strange animals, disguised as plants with snakes inside them. The round plants would turn into snakes and come out and play with other creatures that came from other plants.

I finally stopped moving around in the tall weeds without making a sound. I found myself looking at the clouds moving and then it happened. The sky became another wonderland filled with animal shapes that came to life. The sun was so bright that in between the moving clouds, I closed my eyes and placed my hands over my whole face waiting for the clouds to move back in.

It seemed like a long time but in reality, it was just a few seconds. I could not sit still. I started talking to the clouds. Some cloud shapes looked like animals, angels, and other things like monsters or giants. I started singing, the wind carried my voice as it moved the tall grass gently, creating a wild dance as far my eyes could see. With the wind as my instruments, I sang and the grass danced. Out of nowhere, I felt the ground moving and shaking under me. It scared me. I quickly reached for the ground, digging my fingers in the dirt. I looked down to see what was moving and there it was, a dragonfly under my legs. I gasped! My legs tightened around his beautiful soft warm body. We took flight; his body shimmered when we turned corners.

At age of six, words escaped explanation of how to describe the joy of looking down at the earth from afar and then up close. It was so much fun, scary and exciting at the same time. In that moment, I screamed in pure happiness.

Looking down over the water was extremely amazing. My legs tightened more and my hands grabbed deep into my dragonfly's back, between its wings so I would not fall. The water looked like shiny gold sprinkled with diamonds, sparkling on top of the small wave's tips. We flew so close to the water, it sprayed all over me, filling me with excitement and tingling while shivering from the cold water all over me. I laughed and giggled so loud that my voiced echoed in the wind blowing past me.

My arm extended high in the air, twirling round and round in excitement. Wow! I was so excited but, was also wrapped up in fear. My very own dragonfly. It was getting close to noon; I could hear my mama calling me. I sat up, opened my eyes finding myself back on the ground with shaky legs. I ran into the house and told my mama about my dragonfly but she was busy in the kitchen. Cleaning her hands on her apron, she raised her hand and said, "Not now." She handed me a burrito filled with eggs, pointing her finger to go play.

Walking out the back door, I started crying. She did not believe my big news. Tears started rolling down my cheeks, my heart and feelings were hurt. I could not understand why she would not take the time to listen to me. After all, I had important information to share with her. Finishing my lunch, I went back to my world on the levee. Walking around, I soon encountered a big bug flying and buzzing towards me. I ran with my hand up in the air swinging at the bug, trying to make it leave me alone. Running, I quickly jumped into the tall grass until it was gone. Once again, I laid in the soft grass and cried myself to sleep. As the sun started to set, I went into our house and had dinner with the family. After dinner, I asked if I could go outside and look at the stars. I was given permission, but I had to stay in the front yard or on the porch. Growing up, we lived on a farm, my parents allowed us to run, play, and explore the Sacramento river and its levee without restrictions except for night time. My twin, Mariano, and I lived outdoors playing and having so much fun.

The entire universe was twinkling with stars and vast darkness with different colors and sizes of stars. In those moments, I felt star dust sprinkle all over me. It felt cool making me feel shiny and invisible. My mind raced with wonder and questions. In that quiet moment, I asked my dragonfly if he could take me to the stars. I heard a whisper that I came from a far-off planet. Wow! I really was made from star's dust. At that very moment, I knew I came from outer space somewhere. Even to this date, I have studied a lot to know if it was possible that I did come to the planet Earth at the time of my mother's conception of me. To take human form to help other to understand the history of galactic Pleiadean beings. Galactic being that bring love, kindness, compassion, to teach us love without judgment.

I ran inside, asking mama if she knew about the stars. She quickly told me to stop bothering her with such silly stuff. I ran over to my dad but, he was tired of working all day on the tractor, telling me to go play. I had no one to ask. I was around 6 years old with a big imagination (little did I know that it was not my imagination.)

My house was old and creaked a lot. Tears started to roll down my face most nights. I was very frightened when it was bed time. I cried myself to sleep many nights. Bed time was extremely frightening, the bedroom was dark and scary. I knew for sure evil would come out from that dark closet with green eyes that glowed in the dark that were always looking at me. Those piercing eyes were directly across to my bed. My heart would race and I could not breathe, I would get hot and sweaty under the covers. So, I would close my eyes as tight as I could get them, moving the covers down over my nose just long enough to breath. I would pray or I should say, I would say: "Help, don't let it get me." I did not know if anybody heard me asking for help; I just hoped there was. My mama scared us into being good with the witch that would come and get us if we were bad.

CHAPTER 2

BACK TO MY PRESENT LIFE

Ah, those memories. I swiftly brought myself back to my present life and giggled looking at my wristwatch how easy it was to go back to my make-believe world in an instant. A funny memory came rushing in about the green – eyed monster that lived in the closet. I was around eight years old and still laugh when my father explained about his old pocket watch that would glow in the dark. He told me it was his railroad watch. It had green numbers specially made to glow in the dark, so when he worked into the night on the railroad tracks, he could see the time. Every night, he would put his pocket watch on a hanger placing it in the closet when he got ready for bed. Hearing what he said still did not make sense to me because, I thought for years that the ghost of the lady and the child also came out through the closet to escape the evil that lived there. Even though my father explained about his old pocket watch, it wasn't until I was old enough to understand that it was a pocket watch that use to glow in the dark, not something evil. Funny how easy my imagination worked overtime. Fear and being unsure, and doubt of my abilities was created from my mother's way to control us.

When I finally fell asleep, my dragonfly would visit me and whisper in my ear. Sometimes, I would remember but the older I became I did not remember. I knew he would come in my sleep, but I did not recall all the words or where we went. Then one night, I heard that voice promising to take me to the universe when I was ready and before he left, he whispered again, "You are from the universe."

That promise stayed with me into adulthood and even to this day, I am curious about life and the universe still feeling totally connected. That inner child still lives and comes out to play, inspiring my art work, enjoying mother earth, with all her beauty and all her life. Right alongside earth, with the universe and its vast beauty and mystery, I still fly on the wings of my dragonfly when I go into meditation and touch all those energies.

Sometime before becoming a teenager, I exchanged my dragonfly for riding eagles and soaring high above the earth and into the heavens. It was from this point of view that I could see into any house and all its content and people occupying every house or country I wanted to visit. I would peek in on family and friends and ask them how they were or simply gave a spiritual hello with lots of love. Later as an adult, I realized that the eagle was one of my spirit animal totems. I have four spirit animals as well as and accented masters. When I became a Reiki Master/Teacher, I learned about the accented master, I met when I was very Young. Life is interesting for sure.

It was exciting and fun to see the array of different kinds and colors of trees from above. There, laid before me, were so many different types of leaves dancing. The rivers, winding at times, resembled shining snakes turning into vast oceans.

Moving water into tall white caps, mountains, deserts, cities, people and homes with different shapes of roof tops with bright colors.

I would not stay up too long because it was cold. The high-altitude air up was brisk, and it was difficult to breathe. I promised myself someday when I was all grown up I would visit every beautiful colorful place on this planet. Little did I know about how big this planet really was, and every inch was just as beautiful and colorful. As a child, I was determined to visit the whole planet. Indeed, dreams!

I would not discover until years later that these experiences were not created from just my imagination. Closing my eyes, opened my third eye. This was the beginning of understanding higher knowledge was given to me before birth and how the gateway straight into my mother's womb happened. *Magical creative intuition.* That intuition is divine power of our soul. Shooting through space and stars when the atom split, I landed directly into my mama's womb; fully knowing, I picked her womb for my mother.

I was encoded with all the knowledge from my source, My Higher self, that I would need on earth. Learning how to use this great spiritual psychic ability was challenging. My journey took me years well into my late forty's before I fully understand all me ability.

I did not ride my dragonfly or eagle as often when I discovered how to use my ability to go anywhere, walk, visit, or touch a person anywhere on this planet. The one technical name for this ability is remote viewing. This was just one of my abilities. I later studied how to tune it and learned how much more was involved in this gift. Discovering myself but without a road map was not easy, but it was an amazingly great journey (as a child viewing all this from the Sacramento levee). However, only an education validated it.

As a child, everything is possible; minds are pure and unpolluted. At a young age, I could see energy flowing from all life. When animal or human transitioned, I could see the life force leave their bodies. Energy and auras are remarkable indeed.

Auras are so beautiful, bright, and tell many stories of the life of a person, animal and plant. Humans have the most color around them because they have more emotions that create different colors. I could not understand why others did not see what I saw.

As a child, not being believed or understood was heart wrenching that carried into adulthood. Doubt covered me like a pitch dark night;not being able to see and very slowly becoming what others were saying about me. That transferred over time how I modeled myself into an image of who I thought others wanted me to be - a programed robot.

My vision, heart, emotions, or my brain could not see, to manage the landscape around me. Not being able to see through that darkness without light created fear that became overwhelming. Fear of not understanding what truth was. Truth, difficult to see in the dark, stayed with me for a long time. When you don't quite understand what truth means.

Looking at my great-grandson, I see pure creative truth. On this new day after his birthday, I now go into a deep mediation within my higher self, to bring that child back out to play.

Knowledge was the light that allowed me to see myself-- how perfect my birth and my life purpose were-- and my fear disappeared. *Fear destroys perception.* A human is what it thinks, when you think love, you are love and powerful- a whole powerful conscious being. Awareness, how all life begins is from gemmation (plants) and sperm. All life (humans and animals) starts the same way. As a whole, we are all connected in the same way. All animals and humans have a uterus. Plants have seed and the earth is the uterus.

Now all I have to do is meditate, and I can be that pure child playing with the earth and all her wonderful creations. Ask questions and receive the answers from a higher truth within and surrender to divine power. This is where my art and writing comes to life. I leave it to my guilds.

Speaking about childhood memories, I was outside on my patio when a big bumblebee buzzed by me. "Wow" I jumped up and ran in the house. I laughed at myself and immediately said, "They still scare me." I looked out the windows and the door making sure the bumblebee was gone. The coast was clear and I continued enjoying my morning outdoors. Enjoying many different birds feeding off the bugs around all the trees. All the different insects stopping on the flowers that were in full bloom brought me much pleasure. Every day the trees unfolded their beautiful magnificent leaves into the most brilliant different colors of green. The grass smelled sweet, and plants were beginning to break up through the dirt reaching towards the sun after days of rain, after a long winter. Nature is so ridiculously beautiful and smells better than any perfume. To this day, my love of being outdoors enjoying mother nature and all her beautiful flowers, trees, animals all year around as she shows all of us the spectacular perfection of earth is my favorite thing to do.

CHAPTER 3

WITHOUT FILTERS

Many years have passed since I took a look into my world as a five-year-old. I was raised with no rules. I lived in my own world and played on my levee and the fields around our farm-- even on my neighbor's fields-- just as wild as a jack rabbit. I did not have to help my mama in the kitchen until I was about 10 years old. I had all my make-believe friends (spirits) to play with. Besides, I was too young and only got under foot, and mama would tell me to go play and stay out of her way. That world of pure joy and innocence would change my life forever when I started school around the age 7 years old.

Growing up on a farm, my father worked for different farmers driving a Cat tractor plowing, planting, and then tilling the fields for years. He did not make much money and our family was large. Five children and my mama to take care of. We always had food on the table and for me at that young age, life was great and I was happy. I had everything in the world.

My father had a 1936 Chevrolet car for years. I learned how to drive in that car. I got my driver's license after my father bought a new Chevy in 1956. The whole family always went into Sacramento, shopping and take in a movie twice a month. Inside our home we had one couch, one radio and in the kitchen, we had a long table that looked like a picnic table with a wooden bench. We had a firewood burning black stove. Around the age of 12, we bought a new propane stove. Our bedroom was just as bare with just a bed and one dresser, with so much room to run around and play, and our voice would echo "Wait" I am getting ahead of myself; I will come back to this part of me childhood.

Closing my eyes in 2018, I went into a deep mediation. I once again, was transported back in time. It was not long before I was watching myself playing on my beloved levee. This time I was at the water's edge of the Sacramento River. The ground was cold on my behind, and the water level was high from the spring run-off, moving swiftly. I stuck my feet in the water and quickly pulled them back out, that water was so cold. I laughed and yelled "Ouch," all at the same time. I was determined to get my feet in the water. I grabbed what grass I could find on my muddy shore near the water's edge so I could move closer, I slowly put the soles of my feet on top of the water. Then, I slowly put me feet in a little deeper until I got used to the icy water-- bad Idea. With my feet in the water, I was so cold and shivering; I quickly moved up to the top of the levee into the sun. I lay down on the tall grass enjoying the warm sun. The wind picked up a little and as it passed over me, I could hear it singing.

I started to sing right along with the wind, suddenly insects were flying around me, and they started singing right along with me and the fairies. It was not long before I heard a whole orchestra. Some of insects did not make sounds but they joined us with their beautiful colors flashing while dancing. To this day, I still listen to the insect's orchestra when the crickets and the frogs sing in the evening.

After my feet were warm, I went back to the edge of the water, but this time I just watched the fish. There were different kinds of fish that would swim up to the edge of the mud, putting their little mouth out of the water to take in air and eat. The carps were very big with shinny bodies. When the sunlight hit them, it created the color of the rainbow that fascinated me. The minnows where tiny fish that moved swiftly; I loved chasing them up and down the river's edge, close to the water. I did not know how to swim yet, so I was aware not to get too close while running. I sang and played for hours with the fish under the cotton wood trees. Those cottonwoods, when the wind blew little pieces of the cotton, would float looking like it was snowing. Is it possible for a child to be psychic? Yes and yes. Children are fearless in their natural state. They have no fear or filters; they are fearless little energy beings living in the present moment. No worries; no rules, only pure loving hearts, enjoying and playing with all living Creatures. Everything on this planet is pure energy, making everything on earth great friends. After about half an hour into my meditation I came back and just relaxed into my memoires

Yes, as a child I saw and played with the elementals--spirits and plants that talked to me. All creatures were different sizes that were bright with many colors or just shiny. All were different sizes and shapes that I called my friends. Children see spirits because no one has told them that they are not real and have no understanding when told that their world in not real.

My world as a child was fun and I did not know there was another world outside my home and my levee that was filled with friends that belonged to Mother Earth. I did not have any sense of time; time did not exist. I saw this in my Great-grandson, Charles.

My favorite friends were the tall weeds that would talk to me and sing along with me. Some weeds were tall, round, and had spaced ridges all the way to the top. I was sure there were animal babies inside them, and I would wait for them to come out and play. Every morning, I would run out to the levee and look to see if the little creatures came out. Next to them were these little flowers that were yellow and had short stems, and next to them were the tall blue flowers that looked like raindrops. I loved them because the bees, butterflies, and other little bugs would sit on them. I would lay very still so they would land on me and talk to me. As the grass grew taller with different brilliant greens, their flat leaves would dance in the wind. All around me, the grass gently tickled me with its gentle movement. I would look down at the field around my house, and the grass moved and looked like water. In those moments, I felt I was the only living person on this plant. I knew for sure I was a creature of earth like my friends. I believe all children see what I saw and talk about their great imagination that really is true. As of two years ago, I now have a beautiful animated creative grand-grandbaby girl. Her friends, who she plays with that no one sees but her, are really there.

Even to this day, when I travel in spring and see tall grass dancing across the hills and fields in the wind, it takes me back as a child. I danced and twirled round and round in the grass, that was as tall as me. Loving and singing into the wind that carried my voice among the mighty tall grass; "You see the grass was my friend." My biggest tallest friends were the majestic trees. I had names for all kinds of different grass with different colors and shapes. In my own very young mind, my names for all things were true and perfect.

Sitting back, watching, and talking with my great - grand son playing in the present moment with no filters and now his baby sister talking with his spirit friends and angels were a pure joy, taking me back to my childhood. That beautiful young boy and I have an unconditional connection.

Children have a wonderful, happy, loving view of the world and everything around them (absent of judgement) -- the universe, talent, psychic ability, and them. Spiritual side continues well into their young teens. Life can become difficult when children become teenagers and their innocence gets programmed. They can become confused with their own gut feelings and programming collide. Filters are removed in front of their eyes with new information installed in the brain. Soon, other new conflicting information get placed in our children with new confusing information.

A perfect example is when you go to a different country all the food and language is different and you cannot understand anything. Everyone becomes like a young child with no filters, lost until it is all explained and taught to everyone. In the meantime you wonder and play with all the colors, food, language, smells, senses, and love the new wonder it brings out in you. Ahhh... the experience such greatness that awakes all the senses.

Innocence in adults means that you know that every living thing is connected with the same DNA even if it is just a few strands less. Knowing that truth, we honor and respect all life and especially each other, not allowing others to influence or change our knowledge. "I am source." Source being the universe and all life forms. Children from 1 day old until they are around 3 years old live in the world completely. Then little by little the outside world moves in to change and teach them a different way to think and see and hear.

Have you found yourself not knowing what something is? Your mind explodes with "What is that?" When we do not recognize something, that is a moment of innocence.

CHAPTER 4

LIVING IN THE MOMENT

Interesting morning as I was drinking my coffee, waiting for my dogs to come back inside. With my coffee in hand, I turned on the TV to watch local morning news. They were talking about a lady that was certified after years of studying as an outdoors guild into walking mindfully. They talked about how in Japan teaching wellness was a normal state of living.

It tickled me in a big way because for me, being raised in the forties on a farm, that was a normal natural state of living to be outside all the time playing with Mother Earth and all her creatures (elementals, angels, spiritual guilds, insects, frogs, fish, all living things). My favorite thing to do was talking to the trees, and they would answer me. I always listen with my heart, soul, intuition, and ears. Also, always feeling earths vibrations and hearing the winds singing and smelling storms when they started to move in. Other times the wind was so gentle; it would completely caress me.

I am sure there are still children in this year of 2020 playing with their angels and enjoy playing in the moment. For young boys ages 1 through 5, playing catch, kick ball or cans, cowboys, riding brooms like it was a real horse, using their imaginations, and playing in those places in our mind. Many children all around the world are still in their innocent state using their imagination to play and talk to spiritual fiends. Technology has not taking over all the earth yet. Imagination, creative and spiritual awareness is more priceless then given credit for. That innocence is human's true nature of being part of the whole universe, absolutely and totally connected with their higherselves. As for myself, I can still remember laying down on the grass under the cottonwood trees. When the wind would send the cotton of the trees, it looked like snow around me. Listening to the tree breathing like a heartbeat. I would close my eyes and hear its rhythm. At first, I got frightened at the sound, because I did not understand what it was. But I laid back down and heard it again so I knew it was just alive and happy.

That day, I became part of Mother Earth and learned to hear her breathing. Even though I was hundreds of miles away from the ocean, I could always hear its sound. That day as I played and laid my head on the warm arms of Mother Earth I felt happy and excited to hear the sounds as I laid very still. When I opened my eyes, the grass became tall stalks with branches (the branches were grass blades). I looked up and started to look beyond the blades of grass and noticed all the variety of grasses and weeds with thorns and stickers; they too were beautifully tall with different colors, textures, and smells. Everything smells so beautiful-- some sweet, others pungent. It was a magical jungle before my eyes. I was in a jungle with vines and large stalks filled with wildlife all around me.

The elementals soon came out from behind the tall grass, rocks, and the sandy dirt. At first sight, they surprised and frightened me. Getting up quickly to leave until they spoked to me in a tiny voice. Barely hearing a voice that sounded like a mosquito or a bee buzzing around. Getting very still, I held my breath to hear better, then I heard the words. I laughed and kicked my feet in excitement. I scared them away with my loud voice, so I quickly called them back in a soft voice, promising to speak with a gentle voice. Soon they were all around me. That was one of me happiest day of my life. I asked them if they could send some clouds to cover the sun because I was getting hot. Bam! Their clouds smiling at me.

Another experience that still sticks out to my mind after so many years is when a butterfly landed on my hand and then another one on my nose. I froze so the butterflies would not move and then I saw the guardian of the trees. I could see him standing in front of the tree, but he was not in front of the tree but part of it. It was truly a magical day for me. Still to this day, I see the guardians of the trees; they told me that all life is the same. I have an affinity with all trees, and life. Still to this day, I talk to Mother Earth and all the beauty from tiny insects to all the majestic animals, to the universe. I truly believe in my heart that all children experience the magic that we adults call make-believe.

Quickly going back to my memoirs where I left off. It was getting warm so I stopped short by the water where it was damp and a little muddy. I sat looking into the fast-moving water when I notice a group of dragonflies. I sat quietly in awe.

Looking at the different colors of dragonflies, I began asking them questions. My first question of many was, can I learn your language and can you understand my Spanish. Yes, you can jump on my back or just let me pick you up. Open, your legs and let's go. Sure, enough zoom, zoom I was on the ride of my life. WOW! Off we went in a spilt second. I was flying above the water.

Language was not necessary. It was so magical to fly, talk, and hang out. I know I spoke about this earlier, but it was so magical I still, to this day, remember that ride on my dragonfly, flying over water and screaming. The joy of feeling the spray of the water tingled my whole body. That was alright with me as we were flying, I started to ask question like, are you a boy or girl. That dragonfly and I have been connected ever since.

I stayed a while longer in the memories of my childhood but, it was time to take care of things around my house, like letting my dogs outside and fixing dinner; you know the small stuff. I was still in a very playful state of happiness enjoying the effects of experiencing my childhood. What my dragonfly taught me was to plant the seed of human empathy for the collective whole--Earth and universe because all things are connected and everything has life force that loves their offspring so very much. (Every Thing)

CHAPTER 5

NEW BORN TILL AGE SEVEN

Extraordinary time to have been raised in the 1950's on a farm and not being interrupted with adult programing. The small grammar school was made from an old house for the farm children. The school had two rooms and a middle divider for first grade through fourth grade and on the opposite side, fifth through eighth grade. There was no kindergarten. It was first grade through eighth grade. I was seven years old when my world, as I knew it, stopped. School scattered every thing I knew, and horrible rules were introduced to me. Simple things such as: sit down in your desk, be still, and no talking were extremely painful. So, I would only talk under my breath to myself. Only speaking Spanish became a fear that I would carry for years like so many other children. (self-conscious) There would be a world of challenges filled with many changes, with lots of don'ts, within my first year of learning English. I had a problem with talking and day dreaming in class, coping with my new world filled with a lot of kids and a strange teacher telling me what I could not do or she would hit my hands with a ruler. I was so scared, frozen in fear to say it hurt when she hit my hands with her ruler. My brother spoke up for me and told the teacher to leave me alone. My Mama and Papa never ever hit me, so being hit was something I never experienced. That was my first-time experiencing pain and fear. Without knowing, that was the beginning that I thought it was alright to accept being hit when others thought I was bad.

    I would put my head down on my folded arms and would not move or cry. I wanted to run, but I had no place to go, my house was miles away.

Amazing how my great-grandson triggered my memories of my childhood. I cried for that little girl when I wrote this book, as I could see her with her arms folded in such pain. Looking back at my adulthood, it was painful. Forty years later I made a full circle back to being that loving, knowing, happy woman free of Criticism, very, spiritual and close to Mother Earth. She gave me life, filled with hardships, and filled me with love and also intuitive, psychic, and a healer's abilities. That was a long road, with many years of education and many classes and healing modalities that connect me back to the universe, its many galaxies, s and its entities. It would be years to find and fully understand what a gift it is to be a child and how they view each moment. With no knowledge or programing totally open and living in the moment and full of laughter, silly, happy and creative.

Finding that path forward was a long road and many years of education. Experiences of two domestic violent marriages that took many turns along a winding life. I was born poor into a beautiful family that in their eye's life was good. Being poor was a perception. They had food, a home, car, and nice clothes. My parents had a close friend and had many parties . Life was great and fun. *We are what we think*.

As the bus stopped and the door opened, I arrived at my high school for my first day. It only took a few minutes of walking to enter the school that kids started making fun of me. In that instant, I became aware I was poor because my clothes and the way my hair was styled brought on their razon sharp tongues. Kids started asking me if I came from mars, laughing, and walking off. I looked around at all the kids, and it was true they were dressed very different than me. It starts with small punishments like ridicule, ugly dirty looks, flak, *'what is wrong with you,' 'Hey you are a piece of shit'*, dummy, crazy, these words destroy your self-esteem. There are many other words that create the same sense of self-doubt, self-hate, depression, and shame. After years of hearing those kinds of words yelled in your ear, it penetrates like shock waves into your soul and self-esteem. After trying to recover from those words, the physical blows follow. Somehow you begin to believe there is something very wrong with you. The beginning of hiding inside yourself not ever saying a word out loud about your life. Not ever saying one word about your emotions, dreams, knowing so much, but never speaking out loud. Your shame is so big, that you can not see a was through it.

All the suffering I personally endured taught me how to love myself first and have empathy for people, animals, and all life on this beautiful earth. The positive of empathy comes with love and understanding to never judge. My higher self leads my life. Listening to what I am saying and how I am saying it matters. Regardless of how difficult your life has been, everyone can create a new life and become a loving being, understanding how to heal your self and this beautiful planet we call Earth. I only bring this up because it may help many understand how life can look for someone that went through the same harassment from parents and peers. Unfortunately, we all go through high school and find it difficult to fit in and understand. We, as humans, go through many changes, but I say to you, you can be a compassionate person full of love. Where and when the world knocks you down and you had gone through abuse, bad marriages, or parents, you can change your life and be happy. Create your life just how you want it is possible.

CHAPTER 6

THE ROAD BACK TO WHOLENESS

Making a new life for myself. In the beginning of being a single parent again with children still at home, I was already in my forty's and had no skill in working outside my home. I sat down and wrote on a piece of paper all my duties I knew how to do as a housewife. Surprisingly,, I had a lot of knowledge and used that information in looking for a job in the newspaper ads. I applied at Sacramento High School for a part- time job as a teacher's aide. I was so surprised I was given the job. I was the happiest person on this earth. I loved my job working with the kids. The school placed me in homemaking-- perfect job. My life turned completely around and gave me confidence in myself to look for better paying jobs. Once I started working, I felt I should look for better paying jobs. While I was married for a short time of 6 years, I attended a city college and that opened my door to wanting learn more, lots more. For now, that was in my future.

I walked downtown and found the Sacramento County building, walked In, and asked how to apply for a job. The lady behind the desk pointed to a table and a lot of paper hanging on a board. The jobs listed were great, but I did not have the education to apply. I got a job at a gym where I workout at during summer break at Sacramento High School. I made a lot of friends and became an aerobics instructor. I studied, got my state license, and had my own group of people for about one year. I continued to go to college also. It was a most rewarding experience to have. One year and a half later, I qualified to apply and take a test at the Sacrament

Court. Then they sent me to take a typing test. I got tier 1 and it was not long after that, I had my first interview at Sacramento County Court and got my first high paying job. I was on cloud nine.

That was the happiest moment of my life. Not having to worry about money any longer, that would give me money to take more classes. Take care of my young son, house payments, and I bought myself a new car. Great accomplishment all by myself. It was not easy, but working hard to make it happen was empowering. Truly, I must say that, this is when my life begun. There would be many classes I would sign up for that were available. Also, workshops, at the college and several years of studying many modalities. The healing classes are the ones that peaked my interest the most.

In the meantime, thinking back before my divorce, I finally built up enough courage to go out to a night club by myself. Taking a deep breath, locked my car, and walked in. Speaking about being nervous and scared all at the same time. My family always told me, "Good women do not go to clubs by themselves." Finding a stool open at the bar, I sat down. I was tapping my foot to the beat of the music when a tall man sat on the bar stool next to me. As the night went on, he asked me to dance. We were talking for a couple of hours. Must at admit, I was taken by his smile and charm. Months later, we went out on our first date on his motorcycle.

Months later, we moved in together and got married soon after that. I kept myself busy working and painting watercolors. Watercolor painting got my heart to always beat so hard, I thought it would go right though my body. I was totally in love with painting. My class thought me how to use watercolor paint, paper, and many techniques and from there, I totally fell in love with painting. I was in many art shows helping my name grow. Unfortunatly, my marriage did not go as well. We both had our own way at looking at life. We divorced after 7 years.

The divorce really took a toll on me. I kept myself busy with work and the house helped. I was reading the Sacramento Bee and saw an ad for a psychic fair. That got my attention, so I took that page out and left it on the kitchen table. The following day was Sunday; I jumped in my car and went to that fair. WOW! That day I got so much information; I was very excited, and I picked up a flyer with big bold letters, Enthusiasm and Joy Church. Under those bold lines was a line that said "Come and learn if you are psychics and many other classes in the same field." Needless to say, the following weekend I was there. It would take me three years to get my certificates. Becoming Rev. Maria Garay for Science of Mind, and also, for psychic and channeling.

Shortly after I graduated, I married Robert Reynolds. This union has taken root deep in my heart. To this day, we are still happily married. I kept studying Meditations, many modalities, palmistry, Hand writing analysis, tarot cards, psychology and lastly, I became a Reiki Master/Teacher. One my most exciting classes were art; I love creating art and making a blank canvas into a great painting. All my class were equally as important. I wanted to exhibit my art around the world Only because it moves people as well as helps heal them and myself because when a painting is finished, it always surprises me. With its healing power of the colors as they move you. I have had many art shows through the years, but now with facebook and such, it has traveled around the world. Many years of studying and developing what on a knowing feeling I had for years? I studied many classes for about 7 years and to date, I am still learning. Learning never stops. To this day, I am still curious and what to know what you know. I love painting and get lost for hours within my images and strong beautiful colors. Pure love.

CHAPTER 7

KNOWLEDGE WITHIN

This is where the visit to my grandson's birthday party took me back in time of memories, of my life on the ranch, and being a wild child with no rules. This is how and when Little Charles' world and mine met, or could say, we collided. It was so simple to remember and see my childhood life alongside his. It was my honor to play with him and share both our lives for a short time that birthday afternoon and many other visits.

At the start of this book I spoke a little about my trip from Reno, Nevada and the visons on my way to see my father at the UCD hospital at Sacramento California and the fear that I would not make it in time to see him. Took me back like I was in a time machine. My great-grandson sparked my triggers of long past memories as we were rolling around the floor in his house playing and talking.

That evening when Robert and I made our way back home to Placerville Ca., I closed my eyes to meditate. I was in what I call my silent space in the quantum field within the universe. It was not long before my life as a very young girl whose name was Maria Garay was running around playing with all her many friends on the Sacramento Levee.

Extremely vivid with extremely bright bold colors and smells, I was back playing for hours before I came back into the room and cut my grounding cord that I anchored to the center of the earth. During these deep meditations, I was able to reconnect with myself, not just remember of my childhood memory, but that child self. The gift my parents give me in allowing me to play on the Sacramento River banks without restrictions gave me that magical wisdom to regain it as an adult again. I still go play and have fun with all these beautiful planet, animals, insects, reptiles, and all the trees, flowers, grass, water and the fragrance that all give.

Completely understanding who I became after all my education and being able to transport myself back to my beginning. I started doing healing classes. I have the ability to help and heal others. I am also very physic so whoever someone sits before me get a whole healing, because I can see all their twenty-two chakras and how they created damage on their body. When I look at their aura, it gives me a lot of information. Yes, I can see chakras and their aura. All living things have auras.

In the beginning, I would travel and work at physic fairs when I was younger. I would do a quick painting of what I saw, so they would have something to look at and help them later. I was hungry to help and that was the time I did not have my own office. That would come much later.

CHAPTER 8

HEALING FROM THE UNIVERSE AND THE QUANTUM FIELD

My life definitely was a struggle to get to this point, but I have this fire within that drove me not to give up. My art work is guided by my spiritual being's friends. They speak to me and I talk to them. I am driven to paint and write my book. I am shown what to paint and my art work is extremely colorful and filled with messages from Galactic realm and the Pleiadeans, alongside the Star Seed, and many other multi-dimensional beings that live in the universe. This is what I saw as a child playing with all spirits and the wonders of Mother Earth. All this was imprinted in me as my mother conceived me. Adults call this type of child as having a big imagination, but they are free, beautiful, happy, spiritual beings who have no programming yet, so they see all energy around them. All life is moving energy, depending of your form. Humans have auras around them with colors of the rainbows. We have amazing chakra's system of 25. What that means is that those systems are higher frequencies? Those frequencies lead to higher self, superconscious, and a look at our souls.

Allow awareness, it will bring you great knowledge and wisdom. We just have to go into meditation to remember. Listen and learn to trust and follow that inner whisper. Going into a meditation can be difficult, but can be achieved. That is where a sudden major insight, healing abilities can be activated. Fear destroys perception. A human is what it thinks. Consciousness sees only as mind interpretation of reality. This is how

Jesus healed people. He brought them into his consciousness where disease had no reality. You are the Creator; therefore, for you have no disease.

I, myself tried many different ways to meditate. I read many books and viewed videos on how teachers and monks would do their meditation. It only worked for me to ground into Mother Earth. I learned how to ground run my energy, bring up Mother Earth energy starting with the bottom of my feet bring that energy up through my entire body. Removing any energy that was stuck in my body that was not for my higher good. Remember, we are energy. I will discuss more of this in pages ahead.

All my education helped me back to that little wild girl that grew up on a farm next to the Sacramento River called Elkhorn Ferry. Amazing, indeed. At times when fear would start to creep in, I go back to my memories of my home on the levee with all my childhood friends and feel whole again.

Life throws awful situations at us in our life from the time we come out of our mother's womb. Depending on parents, spouse's family members, and many other factors that play out in our lives. My life was not different than many others suffering lots of pain, loss, shame, and no self-esteem. Learning how to love yourself, and I mean really completely deeply love yourself. That is not an easy road, but it can be achieved. In all the classes I teach, my only and one rule is love yourself. Look into a mirror and tell yourself "I love you". Loving your self brings you complete clear vision of all living things and answers many questions on this planet we call, Earth.

CHAPTER 9

SHARING MY PAST AND MY FUTURE

I have shared with you in this book on how I finally learned the long road to loving myself and accepting this whole world, just as it is without judgement. There is no magical wand to achieve this experience.

After years of a brutal first marriage and six children, I was determined to get an education to understand how my husband owned me. Yes, I was his property, only did as he wanted or he would cause my children or me bodily harm.

He finally left the state with a new young woman. Without means of money, I found many ways of making money. Collecting cans and bottles alongside the road for gas, worked in the garlic fields for my landlady to pay the rent. My father also helped me with food. It would be about a year before I finally got a job and moved into an apartment across town. That is when I got a job at Sacramento High School. The point here in this book is if I can do it, so can you.

I was hungry for knowledge and I wanted to study spiritual knowledge. When I got a job at the Sacramento Court, it opened many doors for learning and painting. To this day, I have a large body of art work and my writing.

I had a good income, and I went to College before my divorce. I took criminal justice, psychcology, and art classes. I started taking many different classes. Such as Dream classes at the Sacramento River College, Hand writing analysis, Palmistry, Tarot, and I joined the Church of Enthusiasm and Joy. I took all the classes and workshops from many different practitioners. I received my certificate of The Science of Mind, a philosophy, A Faith A Way of Life by Ernest Holmes. I became Rev. Maria Garay by Rev. Jeff Serkin, PH.D. in 1995.

I was about to graduate and become a reverend when Robert walked into my life. That same year was amazing. I have always felt that Robert was my gift for all my hard work. We went to Lake Tahoe and got married. We just jumped in the truck and traveled south for a whole month. It was great, and Robert fell in love with the desert.

Let us go into the meditation, how I finally decided what worked the best for myself after trying many different modalities. This particular meditation works best for all my students over the years. It is short but powerful.

Freedom happens when you meditate daily. This will raise your vibration bringing energy in dissolving doubt in the subconscious and allow you to open up to your intuition and a connection to your high source.

CHAPTER 10

INTERWEAVING LIFE EXPERIENCE TO REACH

All Information about Oneself

Life gives all people on earth lessons, so as a whole we can understand what suffering, kindness, hunger, sickness, loss, torture, love gone wrong and all the different and many kinds of addictions are. The list is long with many other kinds of pain and cruelty. It can shape us to be whole, loving human beings, filled with lovingoneself, always achieving love in your heart forever. That is what and why we are here on Earth. Stand in your truth, that truth is that you are whole and filled with love for yourself and all life, that you have forgotten.

My life was not different than anyone else's. Even though in all these past chapters, I talk about my memories of my childhood playing with many friends on the levee. The reason is because I know in every child, they have a beautiful make—believe world that sometimes gets mixed with bad memories at times. I saw myself through my great-grandson's eyes that transported me back in time. He remined me of what it was like to be pure and full of kindness and love. That day I saw through his eyes and went back in time and began looking out of my eyes once again. It reminded me to never speak about yourself with bad remarks, such as that you are stupid or a dumb shit, you are what you think. Words have energy that travel down to our soul. When you speak to yourself in such a horrible way, you buy into what you are saying, about yourself. Your own words can destroy you. Say positive kind action for yourself, and remember to breathe slow; place your hand over your heart; take some very slow breaths, feeling your heart beat. Even if you never take a class, be kind to yourself and love your heart. Just breathe slow, and feel your heart to clam yourself.

Finding those memories and separating them can help heal and bring forth peace. Everyone that was meant to help you on finding your path will show up. When you stay too long feeling sorry for yourself, you will not see them. There are times when pain and hardship are the best teachers on this planet. It teaches empathy and strength that is a source of great strength that leads to self-love, when and only when you learn to recognize them.

Once we all find that road, it can have sharp curves, steep hills, and oceans to swim over. It truly can happen if you desire happiness, and learn to truly love yourself. Loving yourself is just as exciting as falling in love with your mate. The reward of loving yourself is that you are always happy no matter what and you will find who is meant for you!

There are many people that cannot get to a place to forgive others. They stay in a state of infective mental and physical pain. They get stuck in pain, anger, and hate for themselves and others. When you come across such people, just bless them and tell their spiritual guild to help them.

I say to you when you are in this state, look into a mirror just focus at looking into your eyes and tell yourself, *I LOVE YOU*. Repeat this often until you start to see your beautiful soul energy of who you truly are. Also, take a deep breath before you look into the mirror and letting it out very slow, do this for at least three time. It will help you calm down. When you are doing this, put your hand on your heart, so you can feel your calm heartbeat. It will feel like the ocean wave coming in and out taking away your anxiety.

I personally studied many ways to find my road to self-love and total understanding of why I was born and why I was on this planet called Earth. I experience so much pain and self-doubt. I am going to share with you a small coroner of my life so if you want to change yours, you can start your own journey.

I am sure like so many of you were so kind, silly, funny, loved and trusted all life around you. Yes, so I did not know what happened and how I was so completely controlled. It never occurred to me that people could lie, cheat, and control through brute force and fear. I thought it was normal and my fault. I just did not understand what I did wrong.

I was born very psychic so I lived in between two worlds. It would take me years of studying to understand my psychic gift and living on earth. Till this day, I do not understand humans and the awful things they do to destroy earth, water, animals, trees, and your human life. I have been using my gifts for good. Creating classes to teach many how to use their gifts. I truly enjoy doing healing work. (Reiki Master/Teacher) But I also do readings when it is needed. My guides and angels always talk to me and let me know what is coming my way. No matter how it looks, I listen and follow their advice. It is fun to teach my students how to see auras. Some students can see color and others on a knowing feeling. It is true there are different ways to see and read the auras and all the information they carry.

It was not easy to retrace my steps of how I got so turned around and not knowing who I was. I must say my journey took many different roads and many classes, books, releasing my feelings through my art work. Art is a very healing modality, music, dancing, sports, there are many ways to release energy and see the beauty it creates. I did. I loved running, aerobics, dancing, and yoga.

CHAPTER 11

MEDITATIONS FOR YOUR HEART AND WELL- BEING

Walk with me though this meditation and feel your heart space as we reach the 12th dimension, quantum field, your- higher self - energy field leaving behind the heaviness of our everyday 3rd dimension on earth life. Please feel free to try different types of meditations until you find the perfect one for you. I personally like mine short and easy, so I can do them often. For me personally, I found if they are too long, I will not do them as often. Often is the key word to open your heart to self-love, every day is better for many reasons. The biggest pay off is your health.

MEDIATION FOR LOVE WITH NO JUDGMENT

First: Take a deep breath though your nose slowly, then let your breath out very slowly. Do this three times very slowly. Place your hand over your heart and feel it beating as you take in another breath very slowly (Note: the key here is very slow breathe in and out)

    Now, from the tip of your tailbone attach a cord and send it to the center of the earth. Or, imagine roots from a tree deep into Mother Earth. Bring up Mother Earth energy to the bottom of your feet and gradually very slowly bringing up Mother Earth energy to the top of your feet, stopping for a short time feeling the warm energy that may feel like warn water. Keep moving that energy all the way up your legs, front and back at the same time slowly, moving that energy up over your knees and up to your hip and back to your tail bone. Take time to feel the warm energy. While doing this now that your energy is running through your body is removing all that is not for your highest good. All the stuck energy will be removed. Keep breathing very slowly continue moving Mother Earth's energy up the front over your stomach and your hips, front and back and all your organs filling your entire body to the top of your head with this warm cleansing energy. Breathe slowly and while your hand is over your heart. Your aura should be full of Mother Earth's energy, and you are slowly removing any stuck energy through the top of your head out to the universe to heal. All energy removed has power, so you want to call for the universe to clean it. Then, start breathing in your higher energy self from the twelve dimensions, filling your heart space with love, giving thanks for what you are grateful for. Continue to move in the energy from source, universe down your crown. It is a white light you bring down to heal and finish removing any bad energy left behind. Love. No judgment, just compassion for others. Judgment lowers your vibration. Do not forget a lower vibration really can attract an illness. Continue to move out with the white light all though your body, back down through your crown to Mother Earth to clean your energic body from head to toe, inside in and out. There are many meditations out there. Find one that works for you. This one is one of my favorites because it is easy and fast. Reminder to recall all your energy back to you at the end of your day. (It is as simple as just saying I call back my energy.) Thinking back to where you have been, and clean your aura making a circle around you the length of your arms to your side, above you, behind you, under your feet. This will keep your space clean and safe.

I completely understand that it is difficult to believe that we are just pure energy beings. There is nothing on this planet that is solid; it truly is all moving energy. Our eyes and our perceptions react to what we are told, what we are looking at. That is how we are programmed at school. They teach us with pictures and words that send message to the eyes and our brain, learning what they show us, to be true. Play in your make-believe world as long as you want. REMEMBER, YOU ARE WHAT YOU THINK

I truly hope you allow your children to stay into their natural state of playing in there make –believe world (as we adults call it) for as long as you can and join them. They will reward you with becoming very intuitive in many different modalities. Art, Actors, Musicians, Psychic, Writer, Teacher, and in many other creative endeavors.

CHAPTER 12

WE ARE SPIRITUAL BEINGS WITH COLORFUL AURAS

Everything on this planet emits color. On humans, we call that our aura. Planets, animals, trees—well, every living thing has an aura. I personally can see these auras. I can read people just by the color they show me. I feel their auras as well. The auras are energy center that have these beautiful colors that range from red, orange, yellow, green, blue, indigo, violet, pink, grey, brown, black, and white. Tell me what is happening in their lives.

Like I mentioned through this book, we are spiritual being. We are not solid ; we vibrate color depending on what our mind feels. Animal, fish, and other wild life, flowers have bright beautiful colors; we have our aura. If we are under stress, our aura gets wider from our body or very close to our physical body. When you experience being uncomfortable around a person or when you walk in a house or places and it does not feel right, that is your aura letting you know something is not right for you. All life is connected; we are all the same. We all share the same DNA, except maybe for a few less strands. As a whole of all life, it is where you were born, how you have been taught by parents, schools, cultures, friends, and where and what part of the world you were born.

Your lens and programming are what you need to look at to find out what you need and were your happiness is. The most important thing to keep in mind: "LOVE YOUSELF" because "YOU ARE WHAT YOU THINK." That brings all the happiness into your life. Go on a love affair with yourself as you would with a partner, because you will never need acceptance because you completely accept yourself and others as they are. When you have children take a page from the animal kingdom, I envy all animal life because they love their offspring so much. If you notice animals love their human companions unconditionally. This is why I 'love my dragonfly's and I see myself riding on the back of the wings of my dragonfly in my mind's eye every time I go deep into my mediation.

www.ingramcontent.com/pod-product-compliance
Ingram Content Group UK Ltd.
Pitfield, Milton Keynes, MK11 3LW, UK
UKHW050409240426
12048UKWH00020B/1418